USBORNE SIMPLE

THE
GREAT RACE

Anne Civardi

Illustrated by Peter Wingham

Language Consultant: Betty Root
Reading and Language Information Centre
University of Reading, England

This is Stan Speed. He loves to race cars.

Stan lives on a big farm with his wife, Lola.

Lola and Stan have three children, Billy, Sam and Sal. Billy's dog is called Diggory.

Stan built his racing car, the Red Rocket.
He spends all his spare time working on it.

Sam and Sal like to
help their Dad.

But Billy would rather
play in his car.

3

Today Stan is getting the Red Rocket ready for a big race. But one of the tyres is flat.

4

Billy helps Dad take
the wheel off the car.

Stan fills it with air
from the farm pump.

Then he puts it in some water to see if it leaks.
Lots of bubbles come out of a big hole.

Stan gets out the spare
tyre to use.

And fixes it tightly on
to the Red Rocket.

Sal, Billy and Sam go in for lunch.
Mum is cross when she sees how dirty they are.

She tells them to clean themselves up.

Billy thinks it is fun to splash Sal with water.

At lunch Stan tells everyone about the great race. He wants to win it in the Red Rocket.

At two o'clock Stan's friends arrive in their cars.
They have come to practise on his dirt track.

8

Before they start, everyone helps Stan put bales
of hay around the track to make it safe.

They talk about Herman and Hector, two other
drivers who will be in the great race.

When the practice begins, the drivers race
around the track as fast as they can.

10

Betty crashes into Bert's car and Stan turns over in the Red Rocket. But no one is hurt.

The next day Stan has to mend the Red Rocket.
Billy wants to help him spray it with paint.

When Billy is spraying
Diggory gets in the way.

The paint goes all over
Diggory's coat.

Everyone helps to wash Diggory. They do
not want Mum to see what has happened.

Then Stan puts the Red Rocket away. It has
been a busy day and the children are tired.

In the middle of the night, when everyone is fast asleep, Herman and Hector creep into the farmyard.

They steal part of the Red Rocket's engine to stop Stan from driving in the great race.

14

Diggory starts to bark and wakes up Stan.

Herman and Hector hide behind a big tractor.

Stan and Diggory look around the farmyard.
They do not see Herman and Hector running away.

15

Stan gets up early on
Saturday morning.

But the Red Rocket will
not start.

Stan sees that part of the engine is missing.
Who has stolen it?

Stan has to mend the Red Rocket quickly.
He takes the part he needs from Mum's car.

Soon Stan has the Red
Rocket going.

Mum tells the children
to go and get dressed.

Billy, Sal and Sam put on their smart clothes.
Stan is ready to go. He must not be late.

Stan brings a trailer into the farmyard.
He lets Sam, Sal and Diggory have a ride.

18

Stan drives the Red Rocket on to the trailer.
He is going to take it to the race track.

Now everyone is ready to leave. Stan has to
hurry. The great race will start soon.

19

He arrives at the race track just in time.
Herman and Hector are very surprised to see him.

20

Mum and the children sit in the stands to watch the race. Billy thinks his Dad will win.

Herman, Stan and Hector line up at the start. The flag goes down and the great race begins.

At the end of the tenth lap, Stan goes into the lead.
But Herman and Hector are close behind.

They bump into the Red Rocket and squeeze
Stan out of first place.

22

But Hector does not look where he is driving.
And he crashes into Herman's car.

Stan passes them both
and wins the great race.

A steward is angry with
the two cheats.

Stan gets a big silver cup as first prize. He is the champion of the great race.

First published in 1987. Usborne Publishing Ltd, 20 Garrick Street, London WC2E 9BI, England. © Usborne Publishing Ltd, 1987